Ebenezer Erskine, Princeton Theological Seminary, William B.
Greene

Inauguration of William Brenton Greene, Jr., D.D.

as Stuart professor of the relations of philosophy and science to the

Christian religion - Vol. 3

Ebenezer Erskine, Princeton Theological Seminary, William B. Greene

Inauguration of William Brenton Greene, Jr., D.D.
as Stuart professor of the relations of philosophy and science to the Christian religion - Vol. 3

ISBN/EAN: 9783337235710

Printed in Europe, USA, Canada, Australia, Japan

Cover: Foto ©Andreas Hilbeck / pixelio.de

More available books at **www.hansebooks.com**

Princeton Theological Seminary.

INAUGURATION

OF

WILLIAM BRENTON GREENE, JR., D.D.,

AS

STUART PROFESSOR

OF

THE RELATIONS OF PHILOSOPHY AND SCIENCE TO THE CHRISTIAN RELIGION.

NEW YORK:

ANSON D. F. RANDOLPH
& COMPANY,
(INCORPORATED)
182 FIFTH AVENUE.
1893.

PREFATORY NOTE.

THE REV. WILLIAM BRENTON GREENE, JR., D.D., was elected Stuart Professor of the Relations of Philosophy and Science to the Christian Religion in Princeton Theological Seminary, in the autumn of 1892, and assumed the duties of the chair provisionally from January, 1893. His formal induction into the chair was postponed until his election to it could be duly reported to the General Assembly. It took place on Friday, September 22, 1893, at 11.30 o'clock, in the First Presbyterian Church of Princeton. The order of exercises on this occasion was as follows:

HYMN.

PRAYER, by the Rev. Dr. WILLIS GREEN CRAIG, Professor in McCormick Theological Seminary, Moderator of the General Assembly.

ADMINISTRATION OF THE PLEDGE TO THE NEW PROFESSOR, by the Rev. Dr. A. GOSMAN, President of the Board of Directors.

THE CHARGE, by the Rev. EBENEZER ERSKINE, D.D., Pastor of the Big Spring Presbyterian Church, Newville, Pa.

THE INAUGURAL ADDRESS, by Professor GREENE.

HYMN.

BENEDICTION, by the Rev. Dr. JAMES McCOSH, ex-President of the College of New Jersey.

The Charge and Inaugural Address are here published by order of the Board of Directors.

THE CHARGE.

BY

THE REV. EBENEZER ERSKINE, D.D.

CHARGE.

My Dear Brother:

In the performance of the duty assigned me in connection with these Inaugural services, allow me at the outset to congratulate you and all the friends of this venerable school of sacred learning, in view of the favorable auspices under which you enter formally upon the duties of the chair into which you have just been inducted, and with which this new term of the Seminary now opens. A little more than a year ago all our hearts were greatly saddened by reason of the ravages of death among the teaching force of this institution, no less than three members of the Faculty having been thus removed in one year. To-day we are permitted to rejoice in seeing these vacancies all filled, the Faculty enlarged, our curriculum of study broadened, the endowments preserved, a new and most commodious dormitory completed and ready for occupation, and a larger number of students assembled than ever before at the opening of any Seminary year. In this connection I may be permitted further to say, that to me, as a member of the Board of Directors, the guiding and overruling hand of God has seldom appeared more visible than it has in the filling of the chairs of this Seminary. With respect to your own individual selection for the chair you now occupy, I may say that it was a matter of the most careful deliberation. The committee in charge of the nomination canvassed the whole field of the Church for months in quest of the right man for the place, and after long and patient inquiry came to an unanimous agreement to present your name as that of the one in their judgment best qualified for the position. Their nomination was unanimously confirmed by the Board of Directors, and met with a like concurrence upon the part of the Faculty. And now, your appointment having been approved by the General Assembly, we are here to-day for its final ratification by these inaugural solemnities. Your election having thus received the cordial sanction of all your brethren charged with the care of the sacred interests of this institution, and also that of the whole Church, we have good reason to hope and believe that it has also the approval of the Church's Great Head. Under these circumstances it gives me great pleasure to welcome you to this high and responsible position, and to express to you the sincere desire of all our hearts that you may, by the blessing of God, be eminently successful in the discharge of its duties. Having already entered upon your work for a season, and realized the expectations of all concerned, your future acceptance and usefulness as an instructor in your department can scarcely be regarded as an experiment.

In any such recognition of the prosperity of this Seminary as has been made, or inquiry into the sources of it, we must take into consideration not only the eminent abilities and learning of the professors who have successively occupied the several chairs, but more especially the gracious care of God, whose favor has rested upon this institution from the beginning, and the spirit of genuine piety which has characterized its entire administration. While this Seminary has sought to keep fully abreast of the Biblical learning and scholarship of the age, it has at the same time given special care to the cultivation of the personal piety of the students, and never exalted speculative theology at the expense of personal religious experience. Its entire history has been characterized no less by a diligent cultivation of a spirit of humble evangelical piety than it has by an inflexible adherence to sound doctrine. Here is the secret of its growth and prosperity. And this Seminary, in my judgment, was never better equipped for its great work, nor more worthy of the confidence of the Church at large, than it is at this present time.

In addressing you in relation to the importance, duties, and responsibilities of your chair, my time will only allow a hasty glance at these points. You are doubtless aware that you are

entering upon your work at a period of great theological un-
rest ; at a period when the very foundations of Christian belief
are being violently assailed ; a time when truths long accepted
are brought into debate; a time when the very principles
upon which the certitude of belief rests are called into question. Everything in your department is disputed. Every
position heretofore held is challenged ; every principle is
questioned, and every conclusion denied. In the estimation of
some of our most learned men, among whom may be mentioned
the venerable father of our own Board, the Rev. Dr. James
McCosh, who has rendered such signal service in behalf of a
sound Intuitional philosophy, things are in a most unsettled
condition. All subjects of human speculation require a re-
discussion with a view to determine what are the first and
ultimate principles of truth.*

Be this as it may, while your chair is denominated "The
Relations of Philosophy and Science to the Christian Religion,"
it covers the whole department of Apologetics. The work of
the Apologist was never more urgent or more important than
now. Your department in reference to the more advanced
and much extended curriculum of theological study here
pursued may be said to be introductory and preparatory. In
a certain sense yours is a work of exploration and discovery.
You start out from first principles, from self-evident truths,
from truths intuitively seen and generally admitted—and
assuming the trustworthiness of sense-perceptions and of the
facts of consciousness and mental operations; relying thus
upon those principles which are not acquired by experience,
but which are implanted in the constitution of our nature ;
having this ground on which to stand, and these implements
with which to work, you start out and advance step by step,
according to the most approved scientific method. to find
your way, first, to God—to the knowledge and belief of an
extramundane, Personal God ; and, then, from God to a written,
inspired, divine revelation.

* *Scottish Philosophy,* p. 460.

You are not set here as a teacher of theology or as an interpreter of Scripture. It is for you to show that "the invisible things of God, even His eternal power and Godhead, are to be clearly seen from the things which are made," and that God has manifested His being and attributes in the works of nature, in history, in man, as well as in His Word, and in the Incarnation, life, and doctrines of Jesus Christ, His Eternal Son. In doing this it will devolve upon you to prove the existence of mind as distinct from matter, to establish the reality of the supernatural in order to the possibility of a divine revelation—in other words, to establish the existence of a Personal God, and the possibility, probability, necessity, and reality of a written, plenarily inspired divine revelation, and to marshal the evidences, external and internal, of its divine origin. Apologetics is that one of the theological disciplines which vindicates the right of Christianity to exist. It is the defence of the Christian Religion against all forms of anti-Christian speculation. The Christian apologist has to do chiefly with two questions: 1. Is there a Personal God who can be known? 2. Is Christianity what it claims to be, a supernatural communication from God to men? As all theology roots itself in the idea of a Personal God, there can be no theology, no divine revelation, if there be no such God. Christianity is founded upon the presupposition of the divine existence, and upon the possibility of a divine revelation. The divine existence must therefore be either assumed or proven before you can advance to the consideration of a divine revelation.

By reason of an arrangement which had been adopted prior to your election, the question of Theism, one of the great questions of the present age, is assigned to Dr. Francis L. Patton as its able teacher and defender. You are therefore happily relieved of the responsibility of this important element of Apologetics. Assuming therefore the divine existence, you are permitted to advance at once to the great work of vindicating the Bible as a divine revelation, and to showing the defensible character of Christianity against the assaults of all who would deny its supernatural origin, refuse it recognition as of divine authority, or acknowledgment as the ultimate, the universal, and the exclusive religion from God for men.

I take it to be the general object of your chair to vindicate Christianity as that system of religious faith and worship which rests upon the authority of the sure word of God, and to defend it against all forms of doubt and skepticism ; and its more specific object to be the consideration of the "Relations of Philosophy and Science to the Christian Religion." In these times of great laxity of religious views and abounding worldliness among those who profess and call themselves Christians, when so much passes under the Christian name that is vague, nominal, and spurious,—to say nothing of what is held in the higher realms of philosophical skepticism and practical unbelief,—it is very necessary to define what the Christian religion means for us. It must ever be held to be a religion divinely revealed through authentic agents, duly accredited divine messengers, and a system of grace for the salvation of sinful men. A religion that recognizes neither sin nor salvation is not the religion of the Bible. Nor is it enough to say that it provides a way whereby men may worship God through Jesus Christ. Very diverse forms of religions profess to do this. It should mean at least what Dr. Patton, the first incumbent of this chair, was pleased to say it meant for him, "the full and true expression of the mind of God respecting faith, worship, and obedience." Religion may exist in the form of reverence, love, and trust toward God, or it may take the shape of a thoroughly digested system of divine truth in the mind. In the cases of De Wette and Dr. Chalmers, the scientific form preceded the spiritual and the practical.

The natural tendency of the mind to classify its knowledge, of whatever kind, impels it to arrange its religious beliefs in systematic order, and to examine into the foundations of those beliefs. It wants to know what are the proofs of the divine existence, and what are the evidences of a divine revelation. Apologetics has for its object a scientific answer to these inquiries. The two burning questions of our times are, the reality of the supernatural, and the divine origin and trustworthiness of the Sacred Scriptures. The Apologist's work is to establish the one and vindicate the o*t*her.

Theology may begin with a Theistic theory of the universe, or with divine revelation, which assumes the divine existence. Philosophy, which covers the whole range of human intelligence, begins with the primitive and more remote facts of mind and matter, from which it argues the existence of God and the possibility and authority of divine revelation. It calls for accurate and valid knowledge of those facts, which are the foundation both of philosophy and theology. "Apologetics puts reason and revelation in their true relations. Reason states the problems, and revelation gives the solution." * The denial of the divine existence leaves the problem of the universe unsolved and unsolvable.

In the light of these statements, yours is the work of the Christian philosopher. It is for you to find out whether a Theistic conception of the universe has a valid basis of facts, and a valid knowledge of those facts on which to rest. "The Bible appeals to the intelligence of man for its acceptance, subjecting to rational tests not only its evidences, but also its teachings. The full breadth of the argument in exposition and defence of Christianity is seen only by starting from the position that all religion, whatever its form, rests on a rational basis." † Philosophy is thus the handmaid of religion, and not necessarily a rival or hostile system. In getting your theory of the universe, you must combine the facts of revelation with the facts of consciousness; for it is only through consciousness that we can have a knowledge of either. "We stand," as has been said, "between God and the world, and we must interpret both by mind. And, in order to such interpretation, we must have a philosophy of mind." ‡ It is in

---

* H. B. Smith's *Apologetics.*
† *Science and Religion.* Calderwood, p. 27.
‡ Strong's *Philosophy and Religion,* pp. 3, 4.

vain, therefore, to decry all philosophy. It was the study of Aristotle that made theology a science, and the minted coin of Calvin's Institutes such an advance upon the massive ore of Augustine. It was the philosophy of Plato and Aristotle that disciplined the forces of theology, and made them systematic. And "still these sceptred kings of abstract thought control the minds of men, and rule us from their urns."

A true knowledge of mind is necessary to a true knowledge of God and of revelation. The Christian believer, however, who accepts the Scriptures of the Old and New Testaments as the very Word of God, cannot allow any system of philosophy which is the mere product of human intelligence to dominate the teachings and authority of Holy Scripture, or his interpretations of the same. But, availing himself of the aid of philosophy within its own sphere, he can accept its assistance in the consideration of the evidences which go to certify that what Christianity claims for itself is true ; and when well satisfied of this, he can still further invoke its aid—in dependence upon the aid of the Holy Spirit—in order that he may, in an humble, reverent, and teachable spirit, ascertain the true sense of Scripture. But, while philosophy is a good servant to theological inquiry, it is often a bad master.

In philosophy, all consciousness involves duality of conception : conception of matter, and conception of mind. Desire for unity impels the mind to seek to combine these differing conceptions, and either to accept the one and deny the other, or to combine both in one, declaring both to be only differing forms of one and the same substance. While to do this involves the denial of the most palpable facts, yet one scheme of philosophy after another has been built up in this way, on one or other of these two elements, the other being wholly ignored. In all knowledge there is a real unity, yet this passion for unity has its limitations. The facts of consciousness must determine the nature of this unity, and set bounds to its controlling influence.

By reason of the great advances made in the physical sciences and the much wider sphere over which human philosophy ranges, and the antagonisms developed between them and divine revelation, it is the prerogative of Apologetics to keep them in their respective spheres and in their true relations. As the Being of God and the claims of divine revelation have been especially assailed by scientists and philosophers of our time, it is incumbent upon those who are set for the defence of the Christian religion to show the harmony which, of necessity, exists between all true science and all sound philosophy and divine revelation. In the prosecution of this high endeavor, you will be obliged to discriminate sharply between the pretensions of science, falsely so called—against which we are warned in the Scriptures—and science which is based on facts carefully ascertained; between mere hypotheses and laws which are the logical deductions from facts adequately observed. By reason of the increased facilities for investigation, a wider range of knowledge, and better results gathered under carefully tested scientific methods, there has been great advance in the physical sciences. But such an advance does not necessarily unsettle any well-founded religious convictions. The war between hypothesis and dogma has been almost unceasing in these modern times; but, where any real ground for conflict existed, it was because one or the other, or both, were unfounded.

In the consideration, therefore, of the relation of the sciences to the Christian religion, especially the physical sciences, it is a sufficient guarantee of peace between them for all concerned to be duly informed that each has its own sphere, and that the boundaries between them admit of being clearly defined; and that, so long as each one restricts itself to its own territory, there need be no strife between them. The physical sciences have to do with observed facts and the laws which govern them. Christianity does not enter on this sphere, nor in any way question the legitimacy of these processes, and is in no wise endangered by any legitimate scientific progress. This fact should be proclaimed from all our housetops, as well as from the chair of Apologetics. All apprehensions on this score upon the part of Christian people should be put to rest as groundless.

Christianity, however, refuses to be restricted to such external observations, or to be tied down to mere sense-perceptions, and has no controversy with science in her diligent inquiry into the facts and secret laws of nature; but is ever ready to rejoice over every legitimate conquest which is thus made. This is only saying, as Prof. Calderwood has so well observed, "that love of truth, and submission to the laws of evidence, are characteristics of all disciplined intelligence." The simple question at issue between the theological and scientific world is: Is there any real ground for conflict between the historical facts and revealed truths of Scripture, as understood and accepted by those who profess and call themselves Christians, and the well-ascertained facts and laws of nature?

Much has been said about conflict between science and the Christian religion, but little has been done in the way of pointing out precisely where this conflict lies, or in determining exactly in what it consists.

There has been conflict between the false pretences of science and the solid claims of true religion, and there has been conflict between true advances made by science and wrong interpretations of the divine revelation. The chief conflict between science and religion "has been due to diversities of interpretation and application alike among the upholders of Christianity, and among the expounders of science." Such diversities are the necessary accompaniments of freedom of thought, and essential conditions of any true progress in knowledge, whether in science or religion. It has been acknowledged with regret that, hitherto, most of the noise of conflict between science and religion has arisen from a too hasty disposition to charge rationalistic or skeptical conclusions as the necessary result of certain scientific hypotheses, and, on the other hand, from a like too great readiness to infer that certain newly recognized facts must prove damaging to Christian faith. By the one side, certain scientific theories have been assailed with needless apprehension and severity; by the other, there has been too great eagerness to interpret scientific theories as adverse to Christian doctrine, and to do so with an undisguised hostile feeling.*

Christianity rests her claims upon an authoritative divine revelation, duly recorded in the inspired books of the Jewish and Christian canons of Scripture. Natural science cannot legitimately enter the domain of divine revelation and attempt to deal with the problem of the origin of the universe, or deny the supernatural. To do so, it cannot affirm, as some do, that there are no facts but those of external observation, and that there are no legitimate inductions of truth save those which are derived from the sense-perceptions. Philosophy may challenge the reality of the supernatural, and call for the facts which go to sustain it, but the natural sciences have no ground to stand upon when they attempt to do so.

While this is plainly true, it is undeniable that this has not been the uniform attitude of certain leaders in the natural sciences. Christianity has been especially assailed, as Prof. Calderwood puts it, " from the region of scientific inference." By saying so, he meant to discriminate between its being assailed by science, which he holds to be impossible, and by scientific men—men distinguished in their respective departments of science, who yet go out of their way to draw inferences unfriendly to Christianity.

This brings us on to the great battlefield of the age—the battle ground where the great thinkers of our times divide and are arrayed in open, earnest conflict on the great question of the reality of the supernatural. He who goes into this arena will need to look well to his equipment and to the sources of his strength. He will need to have an intelligent and well-grounded faith in the foundation principles of his system ; a thorough conviction of its defensibility and a correct theory of defence. " He must be prepared to follow when the battle leads, as lead it will, into the fundamental question of the philosophy of belief." The field swarms with all manner of assailants of the supernatural, with scientists,

---

* See Prof. Calderwood's *Science and Religion*, pp. 20, 21.

historical critics, and with the representatives of the various schools of the materialistic philosophy, and especially with the adherents of the revived system of Comte, and its affirmation "that we know nothing but the phenomena of matter, and that mind, if there be such a thing, lies wholly out of the reach of direct observation," and its "denial of causes, both efficient and final,"* which leads necessarily to materialism, pantheism, and atheism. The battle is being waged with the utmost skill and vigor. Messengers are flying here and there over the field bearing despatches as to the weakest points for assault and the strongest positions of defence. The enemy is bold and defiant. It is signalled far and wide "that belief in God has been disintegrated by the widening of knowledge, and that accordingly belief in a supernatural order of things has passed away."

You need not, my dear brother, tremble at the noise of the conflict, "nor mistake the boasting of those who are putting on the armor for the shout of final victory." No effective battle can here be given by natural scientists. It is with the critics and the adherents of a false philosophy that you will chiefly have to do. The essential principle of these anti-Theistic and skeptical schools is to be seen in their attitude toward truth and knowledge. They refuse to believe in God and spiritual things, and base their refusal on the allegation, "that the human mind is inherently and constitutionally incapable of knowing whether there is a God and spiritual things or not." This is the arbitrary assumption on which their system rests. "They deny the trustworthiness of the human mind in regard to its normal perceptions, and affirm that its natural and necessary laws are not to be depended on." They ignore the fundamental condition of all knowledge. The older and more ordinary forms of infidelity rested upon the allegation of inadequate evidence for valid belief. But these schools of unbelief base their dissent on the ground that the mind is incapable of deriving probable certainty from all

---

* Augustus H. Strong, *Philosophy and Religion*, pp. 9, 10.

the evidences presented. It is not so much against all forms of knowledge that this materialistic philosophy is applied in our day. Its whole force is turned chiefly against the supernatural and the spiritual, as pertaining to the unknown and unknowable.

I have thus dwelt on these things for the purpose of emphasizing the great need of a thorough and accurate training of our candidates for the ministry and all other educated young men, at least in the essential principles of mental and moral science and in the laws and methods of sound scientific reasoning. And as students are coming to this Seminary from all quarters of the globe, and with every variety of previous mental discipline, and with most defective habits of thought and modes of reasoning, I beg to suggest whether a brief summary of the fundamental principles of these sciences, after the manner of Dr. Archibald Alexander, fifty years ago, is not a necessity, seeing how certain principles of mental philosophy, whether sensational or intuitional, are dominating the religious thinking of the age.

Three things are absolutely necessary in this connection : a true doctrine of belief, a true doctrine of knowledge, and a true doctrine of evidence. To protect the young men from the baleful influence of a materialistic philosophy, they must be taught to pay a due regard to the facts of consciousness, to first principles, to the constitution and laws of the mind, and to the laws of correct reasoning. There is nothing, after all, absolutely new in all this agnostic school of thought, as has been shown by Professor Flint. Sir William Hamilton's and Dean Mansel's doctrine, " that the infinite cannot be known," and " that God is therefore not an object of knowledge, but of faith," has been traced to Kant's theory of knowledge. In like manner it has been shown that Herbert Spencer's system is rooted in Mansel's and Hamilton's doctrine of the infinite and in Hume's doctrine of experience. Good service has been rendered in this connection to the Church at large by Dr. Howard Osgood, of Rochester, N. Y., in showing how these boasted schools of modern doubt are given to the work of refurbishing old weapons of infidel warfare, and to brandishing them before the world as something new and of transcendent strength and brilliancy. The fact developed that, after a period of one hundred and thirty years, Kuenen and his followers, as seen in the latest productions of Dr. Driver, of Oxford, England, and Dr. Cornill, of Königsberg, Germany, have only reproduced the methods and results of Reimarus, of Hamburg, of 1767—and that these methods and results were not new with him, he having derived them largely from Voltaire, while Voltaire borrowed them from the English Deists and French atheists near the beginning of the last century, and from Julian, Porphvry and Celsus, of the third and fourth centuries, Julian having been with him a favorite author :—when it has thus been shown that the same methods had been pursued by Reimarus and his skeptical predecessors as in these Introductions of Professors Driver and Cornill, with parallel results, it reveals the audacity of such statements for us then to be told by the biographer of Kuenen, "that he (Kuenen) has with singular boldness shaken the tradition of Christian piety free from every trace of supernaturalism and implied exclusiveness"; that "he has forced the absolute surrender of the orthodox dogmatics and of the authority of the Scriptures"; and that it has been shown from history "that the only claim which Jesus of Nazareth has to our affections and gratitude is for what he as a man has been and has done for men."

We live, my brother, in what has been styled the analytical and critical age of the Church. We lay great stress upon the right of private judgment, and too little upon what Prof. Flint calls the correlative truth "of judging rightly." The right of private judgment and independent action, while the essential conditions of true freedom of thought and progress in knowledge, yet, if left unrestrained by sound principles of conduct and rightful authority, tends to rash assaults upon long-established systems of belief, and to violent revolutions in civil and social order. True progress is not mere change of opinions, or the uprooting of the foundations of verified knowledge. If truth has been once adequately established, it is to be held fast as of imperishable value, and never to be relinquished.

The new science of comparative religions will also claim your attention. You know its origin and its results. It was a reaction from the natural theology of Paley, Butler, and Chalmers. Its contributions, however, to natural theology, like those of natural history to anthropology, have been of little value. At the same time, this historical survey of the natural religions of the world has borne good fruit, in that it has given testimony to certain well-known and generally admitted truths: 1. To the fact that man is a religious being; 2. To man's need of God, and to his having sufficient capacity to know something of Him; 3. To the fact that a capacity to know God, and actual knowledge of Him, are things very different.

The argument derived from this science against Christianity, to the effect that all these religions have professed to be founded upon divine revelations, and have claimed supernatural sanctions, is of no force. It is one thing to set up such claims, and another thing to establish them.

No amount of assumption or pretension is sufficient to justify the rejection of the well-founded claims of Christianity to a divine origin, with all its credentials and evidences, which are to be determined on their own merits. Over against all such claims are to be arrayed the sources and evidences of Christianity, its possibility, historical character, and necessity in order to the religious life and salvation of men, its actual intrusion into history as a divine force, and the production of a new and divine life in the experience of mankind, culminating in the Person and life of the Lord Jesus Christ as the perfect revelation of God.

You take your chair, therefore, as an accredited defender of Christianity against all who would deny its divine origin, its supernatural revelations, its inspired records, and its exclusive claims to acceptance among men. While the Bible is its own best defence, and carries on its face the marks of its own high origin; while the Holy Spirit is the greatest Apologist and witness to the truth of God; and while the faith of God's people rests chiefly upon historical facts and spiritual intuitions: yet, if we are to go into the arena of debate, and expect to make headway with unbelievers, we must go prepared to conduct the discussion on the basis of reason and common objective evidence. For the individual believer the saving apprehension of the truth, and the inward witness of the Holy Spirit, may be and are sufficient. But this is testimony which unregenerate men are capable neither of giving nor of receiving. Christianity has its independent evidences. It is a divine revelation, as real as that of the kingdom of nature, proved, independently of its self-evidencing light, by its own external evidences, by experience, and by history. We must show its defensible character, and exhibit its credentials of miracle and prophecy, or else it will be in vain for us to call upon the nations to receive it, or hold it fast when received. At the same time, the great means of its propagation is the faithful preaching of the Gospel by divinely called and regenerated men, thoroughly trained and duly ordained to the work of the ministry.

Bear with me, I beg you, for a few moments longer, and allow me to close this address—already too long—with the recital of a personal reminiscence bearing on the subject before us. Some twenty-five or twenty-six years ago, when I was engaged in editorial work at Chicago, on my way eastward I stopped at Pittsburgh for the purpose of having a conference with our late lamented friend, Dr. A. A. Hodge, then Professor in the Western Seminary. I found him in his study, wrestling with Herbert Spencer's *First Principles in Philosophy;* wrestling as only he, with his wonderfully acute intellect and powerful, analytical mind and versatile genius, could wrestle. After the usual salutations, telling me what he was doing, he said to me in tones of most intense, of almost agonizing earnestness: "Either our old-school theology is the very truth of God, or else this man Herbert Spencer, one of the greatest intellects of the age, is right. The truth is upon the one side or the other." This, allow me to say, was before Spencer's great thesis, "that the provinces of science and religion are distinguished from each other as the known, and the unknown and unknowable," and the arguments by which he sought to sustain it—viz.: 1. "That human intelligence is incapable of any absolute knowledge," and 2. "The relativity of all knowledge,"—had been analyzed, and their two elements shown to be inconsistent, contradictory, and irreconcilable, as they have since been here in Princeton and on the other side of the water, by Prof. Flint, Principal Caird, and others.* Dr. Archibald Hodge was then doing original thinking upon the subject. His father's great chapter on the Knowledge of God had not then been written.

And so, my brother, as you take hold of the great questions of your department, you will be called to grapple with some of the greatest thinkers of the age, and to sound the depths of some of the profoundest and most subtle reasoning of our times; and, as you go into the contest with these trained athletes in argument, you will need to strip and train for the conflict, and to be sure to take no uncertain position, make no hasty concessions, and be well persuaded that at every advance you make you plant your foot on solid ground, as much so as if you were climbing the Alps, and that every blow you give is impelled by a clear head and prompted by a warm heart; the one as enlightened by the very truth of God, and the other as dominated by the Holy Spirit. This Seminary, dear brother, has now stood for over fourscore years for the Bible as the plenarily inspired Word of God, and for the Westminster Confession of Faith and Catechisms as the Church's accepted and authorized interpretation of the Holy Scriptures. May this institution ever be in the future, as it has been in the past, the same faithful teacher and able defender of the Reformed theology as formulated in these symbols of our faith.

And finally, my brother, while Apologetics is the general subject of your chair, yet of this you have not a monopoly.

---

* See Principal Caird's *Philosophy of Religion*, pp. 13, 14.

Apologetics defends the truths of Christianity, as well as vindicates Christianity itself. Each of the other chairs vindicates the truth of God when assailed, and especially that portion of it confided to its care. Very good—yea, I may add, very heroic—service has been rendered along this line, especially from the departments of Old Testament Literature, New Testament Exegesis, and Systematic Theology, in defence of the integrity, authenticity, plenary inspiration, and trustworthiness of the Holy Scriptures, which the Board of Directors, as well as the Church at large, gratefully recognizes and highly appreciates.

THE FUNCTION OF THE REASON IN CHRISTIANITY.

INAUGURAL ADDRESS

BY

WILLIAM BRENTON GREENE, JR., D.D.

INAUGURAL ADDRESS.

Mr. President and Gentlemen of the Board of
  Directors:

In entering formally on the duties of the chair to
which you have invited me, let me express my apprecia-
tion of your confidence in me.

A professorship in one of our theological seminaries
is no ordinary trust. Its chief function is to teach and
to train preachers of the Gospel. Because, therefore, it
has "pleased God by the foolishness of preaching to
save them that believe," the position of a theological
professor must be as much more serious than that of the
preacher as the work of the medical professor is than that
of the physician. The theological teacher cannot fail
largely to determine the spiritual health of all the congre-
gations of all his pupils. The low state of p.actical religion in Germany is due to no cause so much as to the
cold rationalism that has prevailed so generally in the theological faculties of her universities. Moreover, peculiar
responsibility rests on the theological professor because
of his relation to the theological seminary. It repre-
sents a system which is on trial. The world opposes
its training as too scholastic. It educates its students
away from the masses that it will be their business to
try to save. The church is beginning to criticise its
curriculum as too extended. The preacher ought not
to give so much time to the study even of the Word of

God, when the nations are perishing through ignorance of it. The theological professor, therefore, must vindicate the educational plan with which he is identified. If his pupils do not become conspicuously able ministers, more than his own fitness to teach will be questioned. The standing, in the church no less than in society, of our whole system of theological training will be weakened, a system which has produced the most blessed results, a system which is the choice fruit of the counsels, the labors, the prayers, and the sacrifices of many of the noblest of God's people, and a system which expresses "the mind of the Spirit."

The professorship of the Relations of Philosophy and Science to the Christian Religion is one of no ordinary scope and importance. It deals with the relations of things, and these are always more difficult of apprehension and more practical when apprehended, than is the knowledge of the things themselves. The nature of the soul or of the body is not so mysterious as is the relation of the one to the other; and the question as to what mind or matter is in itself derives its chief interest from the light that it would throw on the relation between them. It is this that is of vital consequence. Still further, this professorship deals with the relations to Christianity of the things most vitally related to her. The history of philosophy is almost the history of religion, and specially of Christianity, in its intellectual character. At how early a time the doctrines of the Bible began to be shaped by the theosophies of the East! In the scholastic age did not the logical forms of Aristotle mould every truth of the Gospel? Nor has the relation of philosophy to Christianity been less intimate since. Descartes largely determined the method of not a few theological treatises of the second half of the seventeenth century. Even Locke's *Essay on the Human Understanding* regulated the defences of religion during the last century. The critical philosophy of Kant and the intuitionalism of Schleiermacher, the two being often mixed incongruously, may be traced in almost every theological work coming out in Germany, and are appearing in the writings of not a few British and American divines. A large party in the Church of England owes almost its existence to "the airy spirit of Coleridge"; and even among us many of our ministers, and some of them the most useful, are known as Coleridgeans. Nor need we go beyond the sea for examples of the influence of philosophy on Christianity. The epitaph on the tomb of our own Edwards speaks of him, not unjustly either in the sphere of metaphysics at least, as "*secundus nemini mortalium*"; and we know that for two or three generations New England theology was controlled, as the soundest of it still is influenced, by his metaphysics. It could not be otherwise. As Sir William Hamilton, who himself gave the most powerful impulse to one of the chief tendencies of the religious thought of our day, has remarked : "No problem has emerged in theology which had not previously emerged in philosophy." The latter, therefore, must shape the former.

And if the influence of science on religion cannot be traced so clearly, it is not because it has been less; it is only because it has been general rather than definite. Did this occasion afford the opportunity for the analysis and criticism required, it would be easy to show that to such scientists as Bacon and Newton, and many others whom we may not mention, but among whom there ought to be named, in this their home, our own Henry and Guyot, Christianity owes, for her confirmation and illustration, a debt which she has not yet appreciated and which it will be late before she has repaid. Even in the long controversy between science and religion, in itself so unnecessary and consequently so wrong, God has "made the wrath of man to praise Him." In seeking to turn nature against Christianity they have also but opened to her a new arsenal for her defence, a new treasury for her enrichment. This is not strange. It is the Holy Spirit who says: "The invisible things of God since the creation of the world are clearly seen, being perceived through the things that are made, even His everlasting power and divinity." Thus the natural is a true, though partial, revelation of the Supernatural. The natural will, therefore, be essential to the higher revelations of Him in the Written Word and in the Incarnate Word; for God knows the end from the beginning, and each step in His plan of self-revelation supposes those that preceded. If we do not see His handiwork in nature, we cannot recognize His voice in the Scriptures, or in Christ the glory of His grace. Hence, the unique importance to Christianity of science, the interpreter of nature. In so far as she discharges this her true function, even though she denies Christianity, she must unfold the earlier revelation with which Christianity is in harmony and on which it is based. The chair, therefore, to which you have invited me may be said to be fundamental to all the others. The Bible, the truths of which it is the chief aim of them all to present, does not teach either philosophy or science in itself; but it recognizes true science as of divine authority and necessity in its own sphere, and it assumes and so stamps as divine a very definite system of philosophy. If, then, "science falsely so called" or "vain philosophy" became dominant, it is not too much to say that even "the Word of God" would lack a foundation essential to it and regarded by itself as such.

This professorship that we are considering has in this Seminary been held by no ordinary men. It was created for Dr. Francis L. Patton, and after his acceptance of the Presidency of the University it was taken by Dr. Charles A. Aiken. Dr. Patton is so favorably known, not only to you, but also to the whole thinking world, that anything that I could say with reference to him would be both superfluous and inadequate. My rejoicing is that he still retains a connection with his former chair, and my hope is that so long as I shall be its incumbent he will continue to lay the foundation for it in his admirable lectures on Theism. I could scarcely accept his place did I not feel that he would thus help me to try to fill it.

Of Dr. Aiken I must speak, even though what I shall say should be superfluous and inadequate. He is with us no more. He was my instructor in the subjects of this chair so far as they were then taught in this Seminary. He will stand before me as my ideal of the equal union of the scholar, the gentleman, and the Christian. Nor may I pass over his attainments in this department. It would not have been his choice had he chosen his work. He has left a series of lectures on Pentateuchal Criticism, which show clearly where his ability lay and how high it was. And yet his courses on Apologetics and Ethics, while evidently not specially congenial to him, were marked by the accurate learning, the elegant culture, and the beautiful spirit which characterized all his work; and I am bound to add that, after consulting many and more ambitious books, I have often found in his old Syllabus their best summary. Surely you can see that the position made by such professors as Dr. Patton and Dr. Aiken must be peculiarly responsible.

This, too, is no ordinary occasion in the history of the Seminary. We are passing through a crisis unexampled, probably, in the career of any similar institution. Of the seven professors who first welcomed me here as a student sixteen years ago, but one remains; so terrible have been the ravages of death in that unequalled Faculty. The solemn, the oppressive question, therefore, confronts us, their successors and pupils: Shall the work which they did so well go forward? Do you wonder that your new professor, as he finds himself in the place of those whom he revered and on whom he depended, and charged with developing what they began, is awed by a sense of loneliness and responsibility? He could not have accepted your invitation had he not heard in it God's call. He could not go on with his work, if he had not experienced the heartiest co-operation and the kindest sympathy from his colleagues in the Faculty, and if he did not feel sure of your indulgence and specially of your earnest and constant prayers.

The subject which I have chosen for this inaugural address is

THE FUNCTION OF THE REASON IN CHRISTIANITY.

I have been led to this choice by three considerations. Twelve years ago Dr. Patton at his inauguration defined the scope and vindicated the importance of this chair.

For me formally to do it would, therefore, be useless, if not presumptuous. Moreover, as the characteristic of this department is that, while in all the others the appeal is to the Bible first, in this it is to the reason alone : as the question is, not, What do the Scriptures say ? as in Exegetical Theology ; nor, What are the order and the form in which their truths are developed ? as in Biblical Theology ; nor, What is the system in-volved in these truths? as in Systematic Theology; nor, How can this system be best applied to the regenera-tion of society? as in Practical Theology; nor even, What have been the effects throughout the ages of such application? as in Historical Theology ; but, What is true in religion on the ground of reason simply?—it would seem that in discussing the Function of the Reason in Christianity we should, in fact, be defining the limits of this chair and showing its importance. This depart-ment cannot go beyond reason, and it can have no higher value than belongs to reason. Then, too, the tendencies of our age and the controversies in our church render the theme selected specially pertinent. These have been quite as much the result of the abuse or non-use of the reason as of a wrong doctrine of the " Word of God." Indeed, the former has been the root of the latter.

What, therefore, do we mean by the reason ?—Some-times it stands for that faculty of the mind by which we reason or draw inferences. Its exercise is reasoning, and it itself is known as the Understanding. Again, reason denotes the mental power which sees necessary truth at once, without an intermediate process of reason-ing. As thus contrasted with the understanding, it is called Intuition. Once more, by certain English writers reason is used in a general sense for that aggregate of mental and moral qualities by which man is distinguished from the brutes. Very often it is a comprehensive term for intelligence, or for the cognitive powers of man. Thus in the words of Charles Hodge, it is the "cognitive faculty, that which perceives, compares, judges, and infers." This is the sense in which it will be used in this address, except when its employment otherwise is distinctly noted. The question, then, which is before us is, Has our faculty of perceiving, comparing, judging, and inferring any function in ascertaining and verifying religious truth? and, if so, What is its function? and, more particularly, What is its function in these respects as related to the religious feeling, the conscience, the Church and the Scriptures?

I. The reason has a function in religion. Within its own sphere it may be a source and ground and measure of religious truth.

That this is so appears, first of all, in the untenableness of the positions from which the contrary is argued. These are, in the main, three.

1. That of the Agnostic. He holds that knowledge is impossible in the sphere of religion. His creed is that "it is the glory of God to conceal a thing." He worships "an unknown God," so long as he worships. He appears in every age. You meet him to-day, perhaps, more frequently than ever. He appeals specially to Sir William Hamilton, to Mansel, to Herbert Spencer, thinkers who have had few equals in our time and few superiors in any other. Nor may it be denied that he stands for an important truth and because of it. In a most real sense God must ever be "the Great Unknown." "Canst thou by searching find out God?

Canst thou find out the Almighty unto perfection?" The error of the Agnostic is not the affirmation that God can never be known fully; it is the assertion that He cannot be known at all. This denial, so far as it claims to be philosophical, is based, and may be exposed, on one or on all of three grounds.

It proceeds, first, on a false theory of the nature of knowledge. This is, that to know anything we must know it in its essence and be able to define it itself. Hence, as the finite cannot know the essence of the infinite God, and as He is, because infinite, that is without limits, indefinable; we cannot know Him. Would not this reasoning, however, bear equally against our most common knowledge? We discern no limits to the ocean. Yet does that keep us from knowing so much of it as comes within our vision? We do not know even a blade of grass absolutely or in its essence. The little child will ask with reference to it questions that the profoundest scientist cannot answer. Do we, then, know nothing concerning the blade of grass? Is it impossible that knowledge should be partial and yet true so far as it goes? If it is, only God can know anything; for only God can know everything. Thus the Agnostic's theory of knowledge must land him in universal skepticism. If he is consistent, he cannot but say with Arcesilaus, "We can know nothing, not even this itself, that we know nothing."

Again, the denial that God can be known at all proceeds on a false theory of the condition of knowledge. This theory is the identity of the subject knowing with the object known. As Mansel puts it, " *Quantum sumus scimus* " and " *Simile simili cognoscitur.*" Hence, as we are not a part of God, as we do not hold to

Pantheism ; we cannot know God, we must hold to nescience. This theory, however, is manifestly false. Knowledge does require a capacity, a kinship. We could not know God if we were not spiritual and so akin to Him. But knowledge does not depend on identity of nature. If it did, all knowledge, except self-knowledge, would be impossible. To know that space is boundless, we should have to be boundless ; for we can know only so far as we are. To know the non-ego, the ego would have to be the non-ego ; for like is known only to like.

Once more, the denial that we are considering proceeds on a false definition of God as the infinite or the absolute. By the infinite is meant the all ; and by the absolute the unrelated. In either aspect, consequently, God cannot be known. As the infinite or the all, He cannot be known : for to know is to distinguish the object known from others ; and so if God could be known, He would not be the all or the infinite. To try to know Him, therefore, is like the attempt to take hold of something which must go to pieces if you take hold of it. In like manner, God cannot be known as the absolute : for we can know only what is related to us just as we can see only what is presented to our eye ; and so if God could be known, He would not be the unrelated or the absolute. To endeavor to know Him, consequently, would be like the effort to see what must lie beyond the range of vision.

This reasoning, however, though flawless in itself, fails because it is based on false premises. There is no such infinite, there is no such absolute.

There need not be. The absolute does not necessarily mean the unrelated. It may mean that which stands in no such relation to anything outside of itself as to depend on it or be constrained by it. An absolute sovereign is not one who sustains no relations to his subjects ; he is one who sustains only such relations as he himself pleases. The infinite need not mean the all because it signifies unlimited. We may have an infinite line, an infinite surface, an infinite solid. Space may be infinite without being duration, and duration may be infinite without being space. Hence, a spirit may be infinite and yet be distinct from physical forms of existence and even from finite spirits. All that is necessary to his being infinite is that no limit can be assigned to him as a spirit. That is, when anything is said to be infinite all that need be meant is, not that it is not limited in the sense of being distinguished from other things, but that no limit is possible to it as so distinguished. Hence, when we say that God is infinite, it does not necessarily imply that He is the sum of all things, and so unknowable ; it may as well mean that He is a spirit or person to whose being and attributes *as such a spirit or person* no limit is possible. Though he embraces nothing but himself, that self is boundless.

Again, not only need there not be any such infinite or absolute as the philosophical Agnostic supposes ; there cannot be. The phenomenal or relative universe demands the absolute as its ground ; and because it is its ground, the absolute must have come into relation to it. So, also, the infinite cannot be the all. The two are and must be radically distinct. The infinite is a term of quality; the all is a term of quantity. The infinite is the not-finite ; the all is the sum of the finite. Hence, the one cannot be the other. They are mutually exclusive as goodness and space.

And all this is confirmed by consciousness. Its clearest and strongest testimony, a testimony that must be accepted if we are to be justified in thinking, is to our personality. That is, consciousness insists that the infinite does not embrace us, and so that it is not the all; and thus it exposes the untenableness of the last ground on which the Agnostic would take his stand.

2. There is the position of the Mystic. To him God is not incognizable as to the Agnostic, but is cognizable only by an organ other than reason. We believe in God, though we cannot prove His existence. We feel and realize spiritual truth, though in terms and propositions we cannot express it. In a word, religion resides, not in the reason or cognitive powers, not even in the will or active powers, but in the sensibility. Such was the principle with which Schleiermacher overcame the rationalism of Germany. Such, with modifications, was the teaching of Theodore Parker and the New England Transcendentalists. Such, too, is the root of the tendency now so widely apparent to exalt the Christian consciousness as the discoverer and the test of truth, and to decry the importance of everything like systematic or reasoned theology.

While admitting that those who have thus emphasized the importance of feeling in religion have in doing so done good service to it, we are bound to deny that religion is wholly, or even chiefly, a matter of feeling.

In the first place, feeling is impossible without the exercise of reason. Feeling presupposes intelligence. As Bowen says, " It is a state of mind consequent on the reception of some idea." Schleiermacher's feeling of absolute dependence on God implies some knowledge of Him. How could we feel dependence on that of which we knew nothing? Could a child feel thus toward his father if he did not first become aware of his father and of the relation between them? Were this not so, religious feeling could not be discriminated as such. Within the sphere of feeling proper we are conscious only of pleasure or pain. Here the rapture of the sensualist and the devout elevation of the saint are on a level. Of the nature of its object feeling itself gives not the least intimation. As it is its object that arouses it, so it is its object that determines its character; and an object cannot be such unless it be known. "All feeling must be able to justify itself to some idea." Hence, the Mystic in making religion begin with feeling shows only that he does not know what feeling is.

Nor is the position of the Mystic true even so far as this, that there is no place in religion for the logical faculty, the understanding. Because some of the truths of religion are intuitive, it does not follow that all are. The idea of God is innate; the Bible makes no attempt to prove His existence; many claim that the arguments of theology fail to prove it. Still, it will not result that all the truths involved in our relations to Him are also intuitive. Personality is a fact of consciousness; we cannot demonstrate it. The relations of the world about us to our personality, however, are not, in the main, facts of consciousness. These have to be ascertained by observation and reasoning. Thus because religion is partly a matter of intuition it does not follow that it is wholly so. Analogy would seem to suggest that even in it there might be a place for reasoning.

This may be shown to be so even in the case of those religious ideas which are clearly innate. Take the idea of God. We believe in Him because we were constituted to do so. Admit, if you please, that in the last analysis we are conscious of Him. Still, we are all aware that there are arguments for the existence of God, and that the profoundest thinkers have been and are yet elaborating them. Thus the fact shows that we can reason concerning even that which is intuitive in religion. It has been done; it is being done. Moreover, the result proves that it is well that it should be done. These arguments are useful as replies to skeptics. They are yet more useful in developing our innate idea of God. If they do not make it more certain that there is a God, they do make it much clearer what God is. There is thus both a place for reasoning in religion, and it is well that reasoning should be in its place. It will be. We are so made that we cannot help endeavoring to systematize and reconcile the facts which we admit to be true. The question is not whether there shall be theology, but what shall be the system of the theology. Schleiermacher may claim to begin with feeling, but his development is by logic. Even extreme Mysticism is itself the refutation of its pretension. Its feeling depends on reason, and it reasons while it feels.

3. There is the position of the Indifferentist and Exclusionist. It is with the understanding only, and not with reason as denoting the cognitive powers in general, that he has his quarrel. He argues from the sacredness of Christianity as a divine revelation. "It were presumption, it were impiety," he holds, "to reason with reference to a 'Thus saith the Lord.' We ought simply to listen and obey. Admit that what He says is above reason, or even that it is contrary to reason; it is enough that God has spoken." I have called such objectors

Indifferentists, since indifference is commonly the root of their objection. Numerous in all our churches, they do not prize spiritual things sufficiently to care to reason with reference to them ; more especially as it is hard work to reason closely, and particularly in the sphere of religion because of the grandeur and spirituality of its truths.

There are those, however, who make the same plea, but with a different motive. We may call them Exclusionists. They are profound thinkers, as G. H. Lewes ; and some of them are also sincerely religious men, as Michael Faraday. They would regard reason and revelation as independent and even as mutually exclusive authorities. Hence, the latter may be true, though above the former or even though contrary to it ; and so there can be no place for reasoning in religion. This is beyond its sphere.

This view, we must admit, contains much more than a grain of truth. When God has spoken we cannot listen too reverently. It is true, but in another sense it is far from true, that the Bible should be treated just as other books. The question, however, is, Could it be honored, if its teachings were considered contrary to reason or even above reason ?—No. Take the case of "contrary to reason." A revelation that was such we could not respect. We may believe a royal proclamation simply because it is a royal proclamation. We will not do so, however, until we have discerned on it the king's seal, or until reason has been otherwise satisfied that it is a royal proclamation. In like manner, though reason be not called on to try the contents of a supernatural revelation, it must decide as to the evidence that it is from God. Indeed, as there must be some test of this, so, until the revelation has been proved to be supernatural, reason is the only test available. This, however, implies that the contents of the revelation are rational as truly as is its evidence. Otherwise, we should have reason proving the unreasonable, and so stultifying itself. In a word, a revelation justifying to reason, as it must do before in any event it may be received, a right to teach what is contrary to reason, is an impossible conception.

It is the same in the case of "above reason." In one sense, of course, this phrase suggests an important truth. There is much in religion, as in nature, that we cannot comprehend. There are doctrines of the Bible of which it is specially true that we can know them only "in part." They are too large for us. Though we can see into them, we are not able, and we never shall be able, to reason through them. "The riches of Christ" are, indeed, "unsearchable." This, however, is not what is always meant by the phrase, "above reason." Since Leibnitz it has been used by many apologists to suggest that while nothing can be accepted as revealed which contradicts reason, yet revelation may communicate to us what in its nature, and not merely in its extent, transcends reason. The difficulty is not that the truth is too large for reason to comprehend; it is that it is of a sort different from what reason can apprehend. That the ocean is above human vision because it is too broad to be taken in by the eye, illustrates the true sense of "above reason." That oxygen gas is above human vision because it is too ethereal to be its object, illustrates the meaning of above reason in the theory that we are criticising. Now this view is open to the same objection that we noted in the case of "contrary to reason." Indeed, what is above reason in the sense that we are considering is contrary to reason. We would not speak even of the vast stretches of the ocean that we do not see as invisible. Its nature is such that it can come into relation to the eye, though its extent is such that most of it lies beyond our vision. We would, however, speak of oxygen gas as invisible. Its nature is such that it cannot come into relation to the eye ; it is not simply beyond vision, it is contrary to vision. In like manner, there are truths so far-reaching, so manifold in their connections, that they will always be beyond the comprehension of our reason ; but if there were truths whose nature was such that they could not come into relation to reason at any point, they would not merely be beyond it, they would be contrary to it. Between them and it, as between sight and the invisible, there would be and could be only contradiction. Nor may we urge that, as what is contrary to sight may still be found true by some other test, for chemistry can detect the invisible oxygen ; so what is contrary to reason might yet be shown to be true by higher revelation. The analogy does not hold. In physical nature there are many tests of truth, and so what cannot come into relation to one of them may do so to another : but in spiritual nature there is only one test, there is but one reason, we can conceive of no other ; and thus what cannot come into relation to it so that reason can begin to construe it must be to us utterly unknown, indeed a nonentity. Even a special revelation could not be believed, because it could not be accepted, if there were no side of it that reason could recognize as rational. Faith, as we shall see hereafter, is and must be rational. Indeed, it is reason. It is reason acting on the most rational of all grounds, divine testimony.   Its object, consequently, the subject of that testimony, cannot differ in kind from the object of reason proper.   Therefore, to say that the Bible can be "above reason" in the sense that its truths belong to a sphere which reason cannot enter, is as absurd as to say that it can be true though "contrary to reason." Both suppositions are identical, and so the former as impossible as the latter.   Nor does all this imply the Dogmatism of Wolf, that the doctrines of the Bible should be accepted only so far as they have been demonstrated. It is rather the position of that master Apologist, Henry B. Smith, that every doctrine has its philosophical aspect and, therefore, that that only is true faith which reason introduces and which even the understanding can and ought to follow, though it may sometimes have to do so at an infinite distance.

Such, then, are the three grounds on which it is denied that reason has a function in religion : that of the Agnostic, that of the Mystic, and that of the Indifferentist and Exclusionist ; positions the manifested untenableness of which seems to show that reason has a function in religion.   When the adversary cannot make his point, it is a strong presumption that the case is gained.

We will turn now to the positive considerations which prove this to be so.

Observe, therefore, that Christianity is very stimulating intellectually.   The influence of the Bible is not confined to rendering men "wise unto salvation."   Beyond all other books it has made thinkers.   It cannot fail to do so.   The intellect is enlarged chiefly in proportion to the truths on which it is exercised, and where can we find truths which for sublimity and profundity can be compared with those of the Scriptures, "the deep things of God"? Now may it be supposed that Christianity has no place for the reason which she, more than all else, has thus developed? As well might we think that a father would give his children their best training in judging for themselves, if he did not mean them to do so.

Again, Christianity demands and, since true, is entitled to, the active service of the reason. We are required to present even our bodies "living sacrifices" to God. In view of what He is and what we are, it is but just that we should. Hence, the system of truth in which God has personally revealed His highest glory is outraged, if respect even of the lowest sort is wanting to it. Therefore, though the assent of the reason to the truths of Christianity is not so exalted as faith's consent to them, still, it is an assent which is indispensable, because it is an assent which is due. He who is satisfied merely to believe Christianity to be from God, who does not try also to understand why and how this is, insults the God on whom he professes to believe. Anselm has well said : " *Negligentia mihi videtur, si postquam confirmati sumus in fide, non studemus quod credimus intelligere.*"

That this must be so appears from the nature of faith. It is complex. It is the consent of the will to the assent of the reason. It begins with reason in the general sense of cognition ; for it must have an object, and the object to be such must be known. It develops itself with the help of reason in the sense of the logical faculty ; for it consents to what rests on testimony which it understands that it is rational for it to receive.

Its further growth depends much on the effort of the understanding to comprehend its mysteries.   Is not such the child's faith, which our Lord has presented as our ideal?   The little one cannot comprehend what his father says, but he believes it, because he knows that his father is worthy of all confidence ; for this very reason he keeps asking the why and the wherefore ; he understands that his father could not teach him that on which it would be vain for him to think : and as by reasoning he advances in the comprehension of what he had received simply on his father's testimony, his belief in him, and consequently his love for him, grow in strength because in intelligence.   Hence, Henry B. Smith has fitly written : " He who thinks highly feels deeply.   From long meditation on the wonder of the divine revelation, the mind returns with added glow to the simplicity of faith."   And, consequently, a wholly unreasoning faith is not merely a weak faith, or a wrong kind of faith ; it is not faith.

Beyond all this, reason itself is a divine revelation. Human knowledge is not aboriginal and self-subsistent, but derived.   It issues ultimately from a higher source than the finite intelligence.   " Man is able to perceive intuitively, only because the Supreme Reason illumines him."   " The Λόγος," says St. John, "is the light of men ; and coming into the world enlightens every man." Nor is it otherwise with discursive thought.   Reasoning is controlled by laws which God has established and which reveal to us His intellectual nature.   "Our thoughts are not God's thoughts"; yet when we really think, it is in accord with the regulative principles of His thought.   Logic binds our thinking because God is essentially logical.   Besides this, in natural religion, quite as much as in revealed, God is the object of thought. Therefore, He is the author of natural religion, and so it is a revelation from Him as well as of Him ; not only because, as we have just seen, human reason has the ground of its authority in the Supreme Reason, but also because the object generally is the cause of the subjective impression, on account of the connection between subject and object. Thus our consciousness of God is not produced by us, but by God who impresses us. Nor is this all. " God is not simply the object of knowledge, He is also an agent who operates on the human mind so that it shall have this knowledge of Himself." " In the phrase of St. Paul, God ' reveals' and ' manifests' His being and attributes within the human spirit." There is, therefore, no difference between natural and revealed religion as to the source. Both are equally from God. The difference is as to the record. That of the latter constitutes the Scriptures ; that of the former is written on the expanse of nature and on the tables of the heart.

Now the question arises, Does the later of these revelations supplant the earlier? Should the voice of reason be disregarded because the voice of prophecy has been heard ? Such is not God's method. He changes the use of things; He never supersedes them. A revelation still existing, though it had served its purpose, would be an anomaly in the universe. He who knows the end from the beginning has no garret in which to store what He needs no longer ; for He created and has permitted no such things. That the revelation in reason continues, and specially that, as we have seen, the revelation in the Scriptures tends only to develop it, would seem to prove that, as ever and more than ever, reason has a function in religion. All this is strengthened by God's method in the written revelation itself. It has been progressive. It consists of successive revelations. The Gospel has followed the Law and has fulfilled it, but it has not superseded it ; it has only changed its use. This is true even of the ceremonial requirements. If their function was to point sinners to "the Lamb of God," now that once for all He has been offered up, their function is to be "the patterns," and in so far forth the interpreters, of the heavenly sacrifice. And precisely so, if God has given in His Word and in His Son a revelation of Himself which goes far beyond that in nature, the analogy even of the supernatural revelation in the Scriptures would indicate, not that reason was no longer to be heeded, rather that in its more elementary but as divine teachings we should seek light on the mysteries of grace.

All this is confirmed by experience. Schiller wrote : "The history of the world is the judgment of the world." He would seem to have meant much what our Lord did when He said : " By their fruits ye shall know them." It is so in this case. The history of Christianity proves that reason has a function in religion.

It does so negatively. Whenever reason has not been recognized in religion, the issue has been evil. If, under such circumstances, faith has not always degenerated into gross superstition, it has at least lost its power to sustain itself. No spiritual movement has promised more than did Pietism. So vigorous was it at first that, as Hurst has said, " Rationalism in Germany, without Pietism as its forerunner, would have been fatal for centuries." Yet Pietism lacked " a homogeneous race of teachers." Its founder, Spener, had blended reason and faith harmoniously. His successors cast off the former and blindly followed the latter. Hence, Pietism fell. The good which it had done continued ; it itself disappeared.

On the other hand, there is the positive historical argument. Whenever reason has been, as we claim, rightly honored in religion, good has resulted. The Roman Empire would scarcely have become a Christian State without the apologies of Justin, of Origen, and of Tertullian. To the age of faith which succeeded the time of Augustine no single man contributed so much as did this great Bishop of Hippo, and his grand work was that magnificent effort of reason, "The City of God." If the divorce of religion and culture was one of the causes of the Deism of the last century, the defence of Christianity by Butler and Paley and their associates had more to do with the revival of faith with which the century closed ; and their defence was altogether on grounds of reason. If but lately the school of Tübingen threatened to banish the supernatural from history and even from the Gospels, the overthrow of its influence has been followed by new spiritual life in Germany; and this overthrow has been effected by German scholarship. This historical connection between reason and faith becomes most significant when we consider the work of the Church or missions. Their greatest advance has been associated with those periods in which reason was duly employed in religion. As your own professor of Church History has well said : " The age which may be called by eminence the age of the Apologists was also the greatest missionary age of the ancient Church"; and " the great apologetic work in England during the last century was accompanied, certainly immediately followed, by the great missionary movement, which from that day to this has been gathering strength, and is at this time the most characteristic work of the Church." In a word, we have but to turn to history to read the confirmation of Bacon's remark : "A little philosophy leads a man to atheism, but a good deal to religion."

Were all that has been said, however, insufficient, the sure testimony of the Word of God would still be for us enough. The Bible establishes the right of reason in religion. Max Müller is correct when he asserts that Christianity is the most philosophical of all religions. The apostles, our Lord Himself, appealed to reason as well as insisted on faith ; and they insisted on faith because they appealed to reason. Life eternal, we are taught, consists in the knowledge of the only true God and of Jesus Christ whom He has sent. If specific statements are required, we have St. Peter's charge "to sanctify in our hearts Christ as Lord : being ready always to give answer to every man that asketh you a reason concerning the hope that is in you, yet with meekness and fear"; a charge, too, which the general aim of the epistle in which it occurs shows to be addressed, not to ministers only or specially, but to every Christian.

I have given so much time to proving that reason has a function in religion because at the present day and in the Church this is what needs to be established. Our tendency is not toward the sin and folly of exalting reason unduly in religion ; it is rather toward the folly and sin of acting as if God, who is the supreme reason, could be irrational. Moreover, in demonstrating, as we believe that we have, that reason has a function in religion, we have stated the principles which will enable us now easily to answer our second question ; viz., What is the function of the reason in Christianity ? A source and ground and measure of what is to be believed concerning God, and as to the duty which He requires of us, to what extent and with what limitations is it so ?

Limitations there must be.

This is rendered probable by the fact that the greatest thinkers have so supposed. It was the peculiarly wise teacher of the Hebrews who said, " No man can find out the work that God maketh from the beginning to the end." " The Greek sage by emphasis declared that, if he excelled others, it was only in this—that he knew that he knew nothing. It was the avowed object of the sagacious Locke to teach man the length of his tether. Reid labored to restrain the pride of philosophy." It was Kant's design to show how little the speculative reason can accomplish. Sir William Hamilton sought to prove within what narrow limits the thought of man is confined. The metaphysician *par excellence* of Oxford has endeavored to undermine the rational theology of both Britain and Germany. Herbert Spencer, whose transcendent ability even his opponents must admit, holds that man's highest knowledge of God is that He is unknown and unknowable. These are but specimens. Surely such a consensus of opinion raises a strong presumption. When those who have been most conscious of limitations to the reason are those who have striven most to emancipate it, it would seem that these limitations must be real.

This also is confirmed by history. Whenever men have " leaned to their own understanding" in religion, spiritual death and moral corruption have been the result. But two examples out of many may be adduced.

Gnosticism was an early attempt to blend the philosophy of the East, or of Greece, with the doctrines of the Gospel. It would bring the New Testament into harmony with the speculations of the philosophers. It numbered many noble disciples, and it has given us some noble teaching. It was the Gnostic Basilides who said : " I will assert anything, sooner than I will allow a complaint or a slur to be cast on Providence." Yet Gnosticism is responsible for some of the most dangerous errors of the present day ; and though the term Gnostic was originally glorious, it became infamous by the idle opinions and dissolute lives of the persons who bore it. They gave reason free course, and it ruined them as well as stultified itself.

The other example that may be noted is modern Rationalism. Behold it in Germany. Wolf, with whom it began, was Christian in fact as well as by name. It was with a holy purpose that he devoted himself to the study of mathematics ; as he himself said, he would " reduce theology to incontrovertible certainty." He meant no harm when he assumed as his cardinal principle that doctrine was true, or fit to be taught, only so far as it could be mathematically demonstrated. Nor did the evil of his teaching appear at once in his successors. Even Semler, the author of the famous Accommodation Theory, which has done so much to impair the trustworthiness of Biblical Criticism—even Semler was pure in his private life, and little has been written that is more touching and edifying than is his own account of the death of his daughter. But he was all this in spite of Rationalism. To see its true, because mature, fruit, we must look for it in such men as Bahrdt ; teachers who took up the Bible with sacrilegious purpose and made it the plaything of a vicious heart; men who, in some cases, surrendered themselves to the corruptions of the gambling-room, the beer-cellar, and the house of prostitution; persons who, though professors of theology, were the slaves of passion even more than of doubt. Behold Rationalism in England as exemplified in the Deists. Here, too, it began well, so far as sincerity and nobility of aim were concerned. Lord Herbert wrote to prove that Christianity as a revelation was not needed; but on bended knee he asked of God a sign whether he should publish his book, and he believed that he received one. To appreciate, however, the awful moral as well as spiritual results of the "religion of nature," we have only to remember that Hume taught that self-denial was mischievous; that Bolingbroke said that morality was but selfishness; and that even Herbert asserted that "lust was to be blamed no more than hunger." Behold Rationalism in France as illustrated by the Encyclopedists. Many of them were amiable men; some of them, at least at first, were estimable men. There were acts of Voltaire as the apostle of toleration which make us exclaim, *O si sic omnia!* Helvetius dismissed God from the world; but he was benevolent to the poor. More quickly and terribly than elsewhere, however, did the true fruit of their teaching appear. During the four hundred and twenty days of the Reign of Terror "*la sainte guillotine*" destroyed four thousand victims. Doubtless, Voltaire and his associates would have disclaimed these atrocities; but what did their principles do to hinder them? These things were done in the name of Reason, and Voltaire and his associates made reason supreme.

Why the results of Rationalism should be so awful, a

study of the reason reveals. Its own testimony concerning itself is that Rationalism is irrational. This is so because of three facts :

1. The human reason has been vitiated by human de-
pravity. Sin has darkened the intellect as well as corrupted the heart. "There is not that clear perception
of truth which characterizes the angelic intuition, and
which was possessed by the unfallen Adam." No one
has thought seriously and has not felt that his thinking
faculty is unnaturally weak, and scarcely anything is
more significant than the dependence of clearness of intellect on purity of life. Again, sin "gives a bias to the
will against the truth." Men do not like to retain even
that knowledge of God which they have by nature. The
history of religion in general is the proof of this. Once
more, "sin weakens the power of intuition itself." Vice,
and, though to a lesser degree, sin not so gross, must
debilitate the spiritual and rational faculty by strength-
ening the sensuous nature. Finally, " as part of the pun-
ishment of sin, God withdraws for a time His common
grace, so that there is little or no intuitive perception
of moral truth." He "gives over to a reprobate mind "
those who "change His truth into a lie." If all this does
not apply to those who have been born again "new
creatures" in Christ, it still remains true even of them
at their best, that they "see through a glass darkly."

2. Even, however, if the reason of man had not been
vitiated by sin, its function would still be limited ; for
it itself, like its subject, is finite. As compared with
the infinitude of God, ideal man would "be less than
nothing and vanity." How presumptuous, then, even
for him, it would be to hope to comprehend God, or to
"lean to his own understanding" in the legitimate, be-

cause necessary, effort to do so. The eye that gazes on the ocean may be perfect, but it would be folly for it to trust itself for what lies beyond the little circle of the horizon.

3. Were human reason both unimpaired and infinite, it still would not be fitted to solve the deepest problems of religion, or to answer the most pressing questions of human life. For, after all, the one inquiry which will not be suppressed is not, What is God? or, What is man? but it is, " How can man be just with God?" The consciousness of guilt is universal; all religions testify to it. But further than the consciousness of guilt, reason, unaided, cannot go. She knows that God will "by no means clear the guilty"; she knows also that He will never punish the guilty beyond their deserts; she knows, in short, that God will be absolutely just. This is involved in His nature as God. Because He is God, we are able to argue that He will always be just; He would not be God, could He be otherwise. It is not so, however, with reference to His grace. He must be just; He need not be gracious. Whether He will be or not, depends on His will as well as on His nature. The question, then, is not as to what He must do; it is as to what He has decided to do. This, of course, can be known only as He shall inform us. Socrates, therefore, — as he could reason merely from God's nature — was right when he remarked in substance that we could not be sure whether God would pardon sin. Tschoop, the Mohican chief, was correct when, having come to the Moravians to ask for a missionary for his people, he said : " Do not send us a man to tell us that there is a God— we all know that ; or that we are sinners—we all know that ; but send one to tell us about salvation." On the

most important and pressing of all subjects, consequently,—viz., redemption—reason can teach us simply
the supreme need of it.   As to the certainty of it, or as
to the method of it, it of itself can say nothing.   This
is not because the truths of salvation are above reason,
in the sense of unrelated to it; it is because they depend
on what is beyond reason's ken until specially revealed
by God; on what is, not necessary with Him, but op-
tional with Him.

Two results of these limitations require to be noted:

On the one hand, if religion is to spring—as it must
do, to be true—from the reconciliation of God to man
and of man to God, reason cannot be the sole measure
and ground and source of all religious knowledge and
conviction.   As has been seen, the most important
knowledge lies, in the nature of the case, beyond it.
Hence, there must be the light of special revelation as
well as that of reason, and the supreme failure of English Deism is only one of many proofs of this.   Nor,
though not the source, can reason be the measure and
ground of all religious truth; so that, though special
revelation is admitted, it is accepted as such merely because reason endorses it.   This is practically, as before,
to make reason the only source of knowledge in
religion, at least for the learned; and that this less
extreme form of Deism is no better than the other,
is evinced by the fact that it failed as signally.
Nor, once more, though neither the source nor the
ground, can reason be even the measure of all religious
truth; so that, according to the Dogmatism of Wolf,
what has been revealed is to be accepted only in so far
as it has been demonstrated.   That which is too vast to
be seen by us we may not expect to be able to measure.

Are we to believe in the love of Christ merely so far as we can now explain it? Is not the essence of its preciousness that, though we can know it in part and are bidden to grow in the knowledge of it, it will always "pass our knowledge"? As might have been supposed, such dogmatism has invariably developed into lifeless rationalism. He who will admit nothing which transcends himself cannot grow in likeness to Christ.

On the other hand, then, if reason is to exercise its legitimate function as a source or ground or even measure of truth, there must be some rule by which it itself shall be controlled. Where do we find this rule?

In the feelings? Should the reason, as so many are now holding, be subordinated to the Christian Consciousness? Though we believe in election, should we deny reprobation if our feelings rebel against it?—No. Our feelings have been corrupted by sin quite as much as our reason has been vitiated. They share in its finiteness. There is not a limitation which it has and from which they are exempt. At best, therefore, they could be only a guide co-ordinate with reason. They might not presume to direct it. But this is not all. In their nature the feelings show that they themselves ought to be controlled by reason. As has been seen, they depend on it. Even their character can be determined only by it. It is absurd, therefore, to let the feelings decide for us what is rational, to judge that a doctrine is not true simply because we do not like it. This is as if we were to say that whatever is agreeable to the body is safe. Then a man who is freezing should go to sleep, because he feels drowsy. The fact is that before we can trust our feelings in any sphere we must know whether truth or error has aroused them, and they can determine this in religion no more than the freezing man's drowsy feeling can decide for him that it is a feeling which should be heeded. That we do not like a doctrine may be the very reason why we ought to try to hold it. The heathen " did not like to retain God in their knowledge." Nor may it be urged that this does not apply to Christian consciousness. Though to a less extent, it does ; and it is bound to until Christian consciousness has been perfectly sanctified. Nor will the relation of feeling to reason be essentially different even then. Feeling will be perfect because it will be perfectly rational. When God glorifies a man He restores, He does not pervert, those relations between his powers, which relations are so divine that even now in his ruin they may be seen to be normal. Were historical proof of this position needed, we should have only to study the significant connection between mysticism and fanaticism.

Since, then, the feelings may not be reason's rule, may the conscience ? May our sense of right be the measure of the rational ? May we adopt the view so common that he who means to do right will be right ?—Again, No. Not less than reason or feeling has the conscience been corrupted by sin. As in the case of both of them, therefore, its judgments may not be received without question. Indeed, the most atrocious crimes are committed for conscience's sake. The Hindoo mother casts her child to the crocodiles because she feels this to be her duty. Paul tells us that he " verily thought with himself that he ought to do many things contrary to the name of Jesus of Nazareth." With such facts, it is hard to see how any one could, as James Martineau has done, make conscience the seat of authority in religion.

Undoubtedly, in all it gives the unique sense of right and consequent obligation ; but, undoubtedly, too, in all it needs to be corrected as to the particulars of right and obligation. Were this not so, however, conscience might not be elevated as the standard for the reason. Though conscience has a cognitive element, its sphere of cognition is much narrower than that of the reason. The function of the reason is to tell us what is. The function of the conscience is to emphasize among the things that are, merely those which also ought to be. Thus, for example, while conscience only affirms that we ought to obey God, to reason is submitted the broader proposition that God is sovereign. It would seem, therefore, that reason should guide conscience rather than that conscience should determine reason ; that, in the light of the consequences of the fact that God is sovereign, our duty to Him should be developed, rather than that our sense of right should decide as to the truth of His sovereignty. Nor is historical proof wanting, either, for the correctness of this position. No man ever exalted, and probably no man could have exalted, morality as did Kant. Yet, in reducing religion to it, he destroyed religion. He allowed public worship, but only for the recitation of moral hymns or hearing of moral discourses. He permitted private prayer, but only as meditation. In summing up all religious truth in the moral law, he denied those saving truths in connection with which comes the divine power by which alone the law can be kept. Hence, as might be supposed, nothing is taught more plainly by history than this—that the religion of conscience only, or mere morality, ceases at last to be even morality.

Since, then, neither the feelings nor the conscience

can afford the guide that reason needs, shall we find it
in the Church? Because she is under the constant lead-
ership of the Holy Ghost, may it not be that reason
should submit to her dogmas as to what is and must be
rational? Is not the Romish position of the infallibility of the Church, or of the Pope, the true one?—Again,
No. It is difficult to see why the Holy Spirit should se-
cure perfect holiness or infallibility in the Church, any
more than in the individuals who compose the Church ;
and that He does not, is evident from the painful facts
that the history of the Church is a record of sin, and
that the creeds of the Church have, on many and even
important points, often been perplexingly conflicting.
Were this difficulty, however, less serious than it is,
there would still be a fatal one. Reason lies nearer to
us than any other authority, and so no other evidence
can be sufficient to overturn its testimony. If you see
a tree in front of you, the only thing that can make
you really believe even that it may be an illusion, is
that other men, with eyes as good as yours, cannot see
it. Galileo could have been convinced that the earth
did not move round the sun only by astronomers who
could prove, by his own mathematics, that he was in-
correct. The authority of the Church, because evidence
other than that of reason, would weigh with him not at
all in such a matter. She might, by her terrors, force
him to declare on his knees his detestation of his own
doctrine ; but she could not prevent him from saying,
at least in an undertone, as he rose, " It does move, for
all that !" The only theory, therefore, on which the
Church could be claimed as the absolute standard for
the reason, would be the Hegelian one—that the divine
immanence in the Church made her actually and in all

respects the divine reason developing itself on earth. Of course, we cannot now discuss Hegelianism; nor would formal refutation of it seem necessary when we remember that it is admitted to involve such beliefs as that "the real at any time is the rational for that time," and that, consequently, "might makes right." Here, as elsewhere, moreover, the judgment of history is decisive. Whenever the Church, whether holding this philosophy or not, has been exalted above the individual reason,—not merely as a divinely appointed teacher, which she is in proportion to her scripturalness, but as an absolute authority,—reason, instead of being corrected and developed, has been perverted and dwarfed. The course of Roman Catholicism teaches no plainer or more awful lesson. Even the Church must be judged by reason.

Since, then, neither the feelings, nor the conscience, nor the Church can afford the standard that reason must have, if it is to discharge its function in religion, where shall we find it? Shall it not be in the Scriptures? Yes; for they fulfil the two required conditions. In their original form they were throughout, even as to details of every kind, absolutely errorless; and they were this because they are the inspired word of Him who is the Supreme Reason. The original form Providence has preserved or restored in all respects, save a comparatively few of the merest unessentials in expression. Thus the Scriptures afford an adequate standard, and a standard of the same kind with reason itself. They are, consequently, what reason itself, in its very nature, demands for its true development; and, hence, nothing can be so rational as for reason to accept the Scriptures, and proceed reverently and humbly, but confidently, in them, even more than in nature, to think God's thoughts after Him.

We are, therefore, prepared for our third question, which can now be dismissed with a few concise statements; viz., the inquiry, What is the function of the reason in relation to the Bible, or Inspired Word of God?

On the one hand, because of what we have seen to be true as to the dignity of the reason, and the importance of its function in religion, we may affirm as follows:

1. For all that logically precedes the Scriptures, as the being and personality of God, the need of a written revelation, etc., we must go back to philosophy, to reason pure and simple. Even the Romanists admit this. Of the four propositions of the Holy See (December 12, 1855) concerning Traditionalism and Rationalism, the third is: " The use of reason precedes faith, and leads men to it with the aid of revelation and grace." This is evidently true. Though reason is not infallible, yet antecedently to revelation, it is, as we have seen, the only instrument of investigation, the only test. Hence, Henry B. Smith has well said : " If we cannot construct the foundations and the outworks of the Christian system on impregnable grounds; if we cannot show the possibility of miracles, and of a revelation ; if we cannot prove—absolutely prove—the existence of a wise, intelligent, personal, and providential Ruler of all things : then we are merged in infidelity, or given over to an unfounded faith. If we cannot settle these points on the field of open discussion, we cannot settle them at all." Here lies the great and the indispensable work of the chair to which you have called me. Nor may it be said that its results cannot be certain, inasmuch as, since reason cannot discover the truths of revelation, she could

not prove the necessity of them.   There could scarcely be a worse fallacy.   A man may be too sick or too ignorant to find the remedy that he needs, and yet not be too sick or too ignorant to be aware of what he needs.

2. Reason should judge of the evidence that the Scriptures are the Word of God, and so to be received on His authority.   Faith in them as such is irrational and impossible without evidence ; for faith involves assent, and assent is conviction produced by evidence. Yet here for the best results reason must be to such a degree under the influence of the revelation as to be favorable toward its evidence.   Otherwise, to what is strongest it will be blind.   One need not be a Christian to be intellectually convinced of the divine origin of Christianity, but one must be illuminated by the supreme reason of the Spirit of Christ, if he is to feel Him to be "God manifest in the flesh."   Nor is this strange. Careful investigation may prove to you that a certain statue is a Phidian marble, but only the artist's spirit can cause you to feel that it must be.

3. Reason should decide as to the actual content of the Scriptures—what it is that their words convey in a fair historico-grammatical interpretation.   Exegesis is a rational work.   The guidance of the Holy Spirit is indispensable in it, but this is that the reason of the exegete may be preserved from error.   The right of private judgment of the Bible, one of the foundation-stones of Protestantism, is based on this function of the reason.

4. Reason should distinguish among the interpretations of the Scriptures between what is above reason in the true sense of beyond it, and what is above reason in the wrong sense of out of relation to it, or contrary to it.   That is, as a revelation must evince rationally its

right to be believed ; so, as has been seen, it itself can contain nothing irrational or impossible. In deciding what is thus, however, the reason must act rationally and not capriciously. Its judgments must be guided by principles which commend themselves to the common consciousness of men, such as, that that is impossible which involves a contradiction ; that it is impossible that God should do or command what is morally wrong ; that it is impossible that revelation should deny any well-authenticated truth, whether of intuition, experience, or science ; that it is impossible for what reason cannot try to comprehend to be true. All this must be so ; for God, who is the Supreme Reason, cannot but be rational and hence self-consistent.

5. Within the system of truth drawn out of the Scriptures, reason—that is, the understanding—must shape the definitions and develop the creed, so as to ward off error and bring out the truth with reference to the particular wants and philosophical attainments of each age. This, as has been said, is a necessity of the mind. Only when we can cease trying to be scientific, can we, without inconsistency, decry systematic theology and creeds. The Socinian and Arminian position, therefore, that we should content ourselves with the mere statements of Scripture and not go on and develop the legitimate inferences from them, is not only false ; it is also impossible, as is evinced by the notorious fact that Socinians and Arminians, as well as Calvinists, have their systematic theology. Indeed, on but one condition is the course which they advocate possible, and that is, that there has been a loss of interest in "the deep things of God." Hence, the clamor even among us for a short creed to state only the truths indispensable to salvation, is far from reassuring. It would seem to

indicate less zeal for the truth as such and to forebode less efficiency in the service of Him who is "the truth." A great Scotch theologian has said: "No mere simplification of a belief has ever conquered, unless the half has burned more brightly than the whole." Nor may it be replied that the fallen understanding is not competent to grapple with spiritual realities. The same might be said with reference to the manifold mysteries of nature. All that the reply amounts to is that in the use of the understanding, as of every other power, we should constantly seek the aid of the Holy Spirit; and the question may well be raised in rejoinder, whether God would have addressed the Scriptures to human reason, and commanded us to "search" them, and promised by His Spirit to guide us, had He not intended that even the understanding should make the effort. It is the searching faculty.

On the other hand, because of the limitations of the reason, we ought to affirm:

1. Reason may not presume by itself to fathom or reconcile even those of the deep truths of Scripture which it can discern unaided. The fact is, that it has not been able to. As Professor Christlieb has written: "Neither in ancient nor in modern times has it been possible to find in the whole earth a nation which, without the revelation recorded in Scripture and by its own powers of thought, has arrived at definite belief in one living personal God!" And this sweeping statement is emphasized by Plato's well-known complaint, "How can we find out the father and maker of all this universe?" There is a theology of nature and of reason; but even when most developed, its incompleteness and uncertainty demand the full and clear revelation in the Written Word.

2. In particular, reason alone has nothing to say as to either the fact or the method of human salvation. It is even her function, that she may not deceive men, to declare that on this supreme question she of herself knows nothing. When, therefore, God has revealed His grace in the Gospel of His Son, she has but two things to do—to point men to it, and to show them its wondrous harmony with the scheme of nature. The highest function of Philosophy or of Science is to bring men to the cross as to that for which she has ever been seeking but which she could never by herself have found ; and then with them take her place, an expectant reverent learner, before "the wisdom as well as the power of God," and thus herself be made "wise unto salvation."

Having now outlined the function of the reason in relation to the Scriptures, it would be proper to show in detail how this department, whose special aim is to discuss the various relations of reason in both philosophy and science to religion, underlies all the rest of the departments, and how, in turn, each one of them contributes to it. It would also be interesting to consider how this chair should be conducted so as to develop the scholarly apologists who, as every age has needed them, will be demanded, we must assume, by that on which we are entering. To either of these themes, however, an address at least as long as the too long one to which you have listened would have to be given. Let me, therefore, close with simply the briefest statement of what, in my judgment, should be the three supremely important practical results of such a course of study as the existence of this chair supposes.

These results have reference to the actual work of the minister of the Gospel. For the purpose of this

Seminary, we can scarcely repeat too often, is, first of all, evangelistic. Indeed, it is scholastic only for the same reason that caused God to choose for the typical evangelist that one of the apostles of whom alone it could be said, "Thy much learning doth turn thee to madness." These results have special reference—may I not add ?—to the work of the missionary ; for, according to our Saviour's last and great commission, missions are the evangelistic work and so the business of the Church. It has been the glory of this Seminary that from the beginning she has been mindful of this. May I not express my earnest hope that with growth in the number of students and with the increase of professorships this missionary spirit will steadily develop until every influence of this institution shall be concentrated on the evangelization of the nations? The practical results, therefore, to be expected of this chair should be :

1. The formation in the rising ministry of a logical habit of mind. We do not need so much philosophical preaching as we have, but we do need more logical preaching than some even of what aspires to be philosophical actually is. The Gospel, which is the "Wisdom of God," cannot be justly presented when the laws of thought, of divine as well as of human thought, are violated. Indeed, to be illogical in preaching is to caricature Him whom you would exalt.

2. The grounding of our ministers in that philosophy which underlies the Word of God and which is assumed by it, and the acquainting them with that "science falsely so called" which antagonizes it. It is not ordinarily necessary that the preacher of righteousness should spend his time in assailing Materialism or Pantheism, or any other -ism due to human conceit and inconsistency ; but it is necessary that he should be so

aware of the dangers of these, and so skilled in detecting the subtle forms in which they are wont to manifest themselves, that he will never dishonor the special revelation of God by unconsciously appearing even to imply that it rests on any such foundation.

3. And, finally, this chair ought to aim to inspire our ministers and missionaries with such holy and intelligent confidence in both the past and the future of Christianity that they will be abundantly able to vindicate it, and for that very reason will feel that it needs no apology. The true philosophy of religion should convince us that Christianity is "the desire of all nations." The study of her evidences should persuade us that she is divine and her records inspired and throughout infallible, or that nothing is true. The examination of her ethics should prove to us that to behold the "fulfilment of all righteousness" we must turn to the words and works of her Author. The investigation of her sociological applications and achievements should demonstrate to us that the regeneration of society requires no new and artificial scheme of life, but simply the practical recognition in all spheres of the Gospel of Christ. The survey and analysis of the other great religions should establish for us beyond a peradventure that Christianity is the one wholly true, the one divinely sanctioned, the one authoritative, and the final religion equally for us and for all men. In a word, the entire course of study should so set forth man's need of redemption and the inability of reason unaided to provide or discover it, that it shall be felt that the only rational attitude for any one in religion is that of humble, reverent, adoring inquiry before the cross of Him in whom "the wisdom and the power and the grace of God" are "reconciling the world unto Himself."